THE Remarkable Friendship OF MR. CAT AND MR. RAT

THE Remarkable Friendship OF MR. CAT AND MR. RAT

by Rick Walton • illustrated by Lisa McCue

G. P. Putnam's Sons

G. P. PUTNAM'S SONS
A division of Penguin Young Readers Group.
Published by The Penguin Group.
Penguin Group (USA) Inc., 375 Hudson Street, New York, NY 10014, U.S.A.
Penguin Group (Canada), 90 Eglinton Avenue East, Suite 700, Toronto, Ontario, Canada M4P 2Y3
(a division of Pearson Penguin Canada Inc.).
Penguin Books Ltd, 80 Strand, London WC2R 0RL, England.
Penguin Ireland, 25 St. Stephen's Green, Dublin 2, Ireland (a division of Penguin Books Ltd.).
Penguin Group (Australia), 250 Camberwell Road, Camberwell, Victoria 3124, Australia
(a division of Pearson Australia Group Pty Ltd).
Penguin Books India Pvt Ltd, 11 Community Centre, Panchsheel Park, New Delhi - 110 017, India.
Penguin Group (NZ), Cnr Airborne and Rosedale Roads, Albany, Auckland 1310, New Zealand
(a division of Pearson New Zealand Ltd).
Penguin Books (South Africa) (Pty) Ltd, 24 Sturdee Avenue, Rosebank, Johannesburg 2196, South Africa.
Penguin Books Ltd, Registered Offices: 80 Strand, London WC2R 0RL, England.

Manufactured in China by South China Printing Co. Ltd.
Design by Katrina Damkoehler. Text set in Monkton Medium.
The art was done on scratchboard with watercolors.

Library of Congress Cataloging-in-Publication Data
Walton, Rick. The remarkable friendship of Mr. Cat and Mr. Rat / Rick Walton ;
illustrated by Lisa McCue.   p. cm.
Summary: Mr. Cat and Mr. Rat enjoy playing tricks on one another, but they discover
true friendship after one receives a tasty gift that he believes is from the other.
[1. Friendship—Fiction. 2. Gifts—Fiction. 3. Cats—Fiction. 4. Rats—Fiction. 5. Stories in rhyme.]
I. McCue, Lisa, ill. II. Title. III. Title: Remarkable friendship of Mister Cat and Mister Rat.
PZ8.3.W199Rem 2006   [E]—dc22   2005035394

ISBN 0-399-23899-9
1   3   5   7   9   10   8   6   4   2
First Impression

To Josh and Thayne Walton,
best friends and brothers —R. W.

To Paige —L. M.

Mr. Cat and Mr. Rat
lived happily together.
The two were very best of friends,
except when there was weather.

For Mr. Cat loved Mr. Rat,
much more than other mice.
He'd love his dear friend even more
cooked and served with spice.

And Mr. Rat loved Mr. Cat,
every night and day.
He'd love his dear friend even more
to pack and move away.

Once Mr. Rat saw Mr. Cat
before the fire, sleeping.
"Your tail makes such a lovely broom!
These ashes need some sweeping."

Then Mr. Cat awoke from that
and found his tail on fire.
Said Mr. Rat to Mr. Cat,
"Oh, bravo, Cat! Dance higher!"

Then Mr. Cat gave Mr. Rat
a ball of cheddar cheese.
"Thank you so much!" said Mr. Rat.
"But lose the trap first, please."

Then one day Mr. Richards,
an old man who lived next door,
was sent a gift from Mr. Cook,
who lived in Baltimore.

By accident the box was left
at Mr. Rat's front door.
And when he found it there, he said,
"I wonder who it's for?

"Why, it's for me! I'm Mr. R,
which stands for Mr. Rat.
And who could it have come from?
Mr. C? That's Mr. Cat!

"It's probably a trap or joke,
like trash or rocks or fleas."
He opened it up carefully,
and in it, he found . . .

...cheese!

He smiled wide. And then he frowned,
and said, "Is this a trick?
I'll bet that this is poisoned cheese.
He wants to make me sick!"

So Mr. Rat tried just one bite,
then two, then five, then eight.
And when he'd eaten all the cheese,
he found that he felt great.

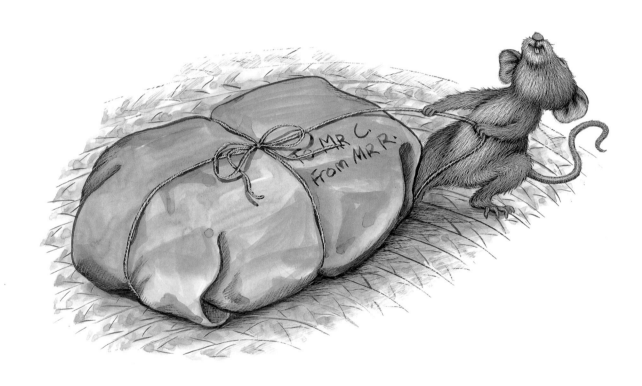

"That present from my dear, dear friend
has given me a lift.
Now I'll return the favor
and give Mr. Cat a gift!"

So later on that evening,
after going out for air,
Mr. Cat came home to find
a package on his chair.

"What's this?" he said. "For Mr. C?
That must mean Mr. Cat.
It says that it's from Mr. R.
Could that be Mr. Rat?

"A trap, I'll bet! What kind of fool
does that rat think I am?"
He opened it up carefully,
and in it was a . . .

...**ham!**

He smiled wide. And then he frowned,
and said, "This is a trick!
I'm sure that it's a poisoned ham.
He wants to make me sick!"

So Mr. Cat tried just one bite,
then two, then six, then nine.
And when he'd eaten all the ham,
he found he felt just fine.

"Oh, what a gift, and what a friend
to make my day so pleasant.
Now I'll return the favor
and give Mr. Rat a present!"

And oh, how Mr. Rat was touched.
"Another gift for me!"
And so, of course, he gave again.
He gave most generously.

And on, for years,

the two friends gave

fine gifts of every size,

although at times the presents were

an extra big . . .

...surprise!